Mum can
fix it

Verna Allette Wilkins
and Elaine Mills

Published by **Tamarind Books**

© 1987 Tamarind Ltd   ISBN 1 870516 01 X   Printed in Singapore

second reprint

1

Kay's Family

Kay

Mum

Ben

Dad

2

Kay's Friends

Joanna

Danny

Danny's mum

The cat

3

Ben and Kay were playing
hide and seek
with Danny and Joanna.

'It's time to go home,'
their mother said.
'Oh, no!' said Kay.
'Oh, yes!' said Mum.

'Why do we have to go?'
asked Ben.

Look at the time!
It's three o'clock.

'Your dad is coming home
at five o'clock,' said Mum,
'and we have his key.
We must get home by five
to let him in.'

'Wave goodbye!'

Time to go!
It's five past three.

They drove along the motorway
and then turned off.

'Look out!' said Ben. 'The load
on that lorry is not safe.'
'No,' said Mum. She pressed
her foot on the brake to slow
the car down and then . . .

A crate fell off the lorry
and smashed to bits.

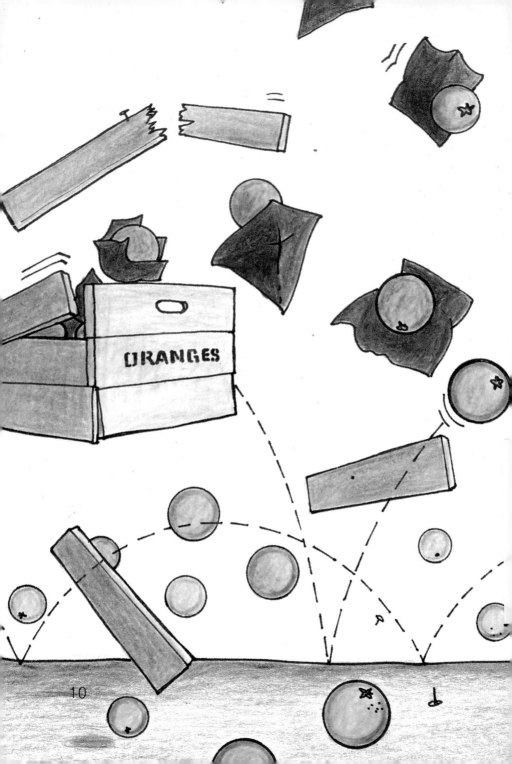

Bang! Wallop! Snap!
Oranges were rolling
everywhere.
Purple papers flew
like crazy kites.

Then they felt a sudden bump.
'What was that?' asked Kay.
A noise was coming
from beneath the car.

Kay and Ben were scared.

Mum steered the car
into a layby just ahead
and stopped quickly.
Other cars were stopping too.

On the road
were lots of oranges.
Some were squashed as flat
as pancakes.

Mum put the handbrake on
and turned the engine off.

'Sit still!' she said,
'I shall have to look at the car.
There is something wrong!'

It's half past three. We may be late.

What has gone wrong
with the car?

'Can we still get home
in time for Dad?' asked Kay.
'Yes,' said Mum, 'I think we can.
The tyre is flat, but we can fix it.'

'All the tools we need
are in the boot.'

This is what they saw inside the boot.

Two blocks to hold the car

One jack to lift the car

A wrench to loosen the nuts on the wheel

One spare wheel

'Stand over here by me,'
said Mum, 'and watch.'

'This is how to change
the wheel.'

1. Safety first

Turn on the flashing lights.
Make sure the car is safe and
cannot roll away.

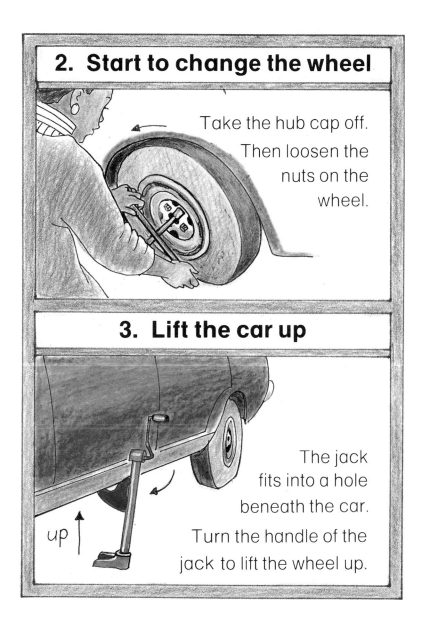

2. Start to change the wheel

Take the hub cap off.
Then loosen the
nuts on the
wheel.

3. Lift the car up

The jack
fits into a hole
beneath the car.
Turn the handle of the
jack to lift the wheel up.

up

4. Take the wheel off

Take off the nuts
and remove
the wheel.

5. Put the spare wheel on

Fit the spare wheel
onto the car and
then put back
the nuts.

6. Lower the car

Turn the handle
of the jack
until the wheel
is down on
the road.

7. Make sure the wheel is safe

Turn the nuts
until they are
very tight
and put the
hubcap back.

Ben got hold of the wheel
that Mum had taken off.

'Look! There is a nail
in the tyre,' he said.

'The nail fell off the lorry.
That's how we got a puncture.'

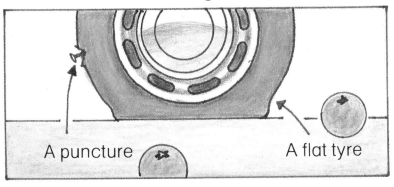

A puncture   A flat tyre

'Yes,' said Mum. 'That's right.
The nail made a hole and the air
inside the tyre blew out.'

They put the wheel
into the boot with all the tools.

'There!' said Mum. 'We did it.'
Kay and Ben began to clap.

'No time for that,' said Mum.
'Get into the car! Be quick!
We've got to get home
by five o'clock!'

Look at the time!

It is quarter past four.

Just then a yellow van
pulled up. A man got out.
'I see your flashing lights
are on,' he said.
'Do you need any help?'

'No, but thank you.'
Mum replied.
'We changed a wheel and now
we have to go.'

'Mum has fixed it!' Kay called
out as the car drove off.

She was very proud.

The car drove into the road
where the family lived.

'Home at last!' said Ben.
'Is Dad outside the door?'

'No, not yet,' said Mum.
'Have a look at the time.
It's five o'clock.'

Home on time at five o'clock

Dad had missed the bus.
He didn't get home
for half an hour.

Dad was late at half past five.

Ben and Kay told Dad
all about the horrid old lorry
and the car. They told him
how Mum fixed it.

Dad was very pleased.

After tea they all
played hide and seek
until it was time for bed.